HENRY

FRIGHT
NIGHT

AT THE AGE OF EIGHT. SHE WROTE HORRID HENRY BOOK IN 1994. HORRID HENRY GONE ON TO CONQUER THE GLOBE; HIS ADVENTURES HAVE SOLD MILLIONS OF COPIES WORLDWIDE.

FRANCESCA HAS WON THE CHILDREN'S BOOK OF THE YEAR AWARD AND IN 2009 WAS AWARDED A GOLD BLUE PETER BADGE. SHE WAS ALSO A TRUSTEE OF THE WORLD BOOK DAY CHARITY FOR SIX YEARS.

FRANCESCA LIVES IN NORTH LONDON WITH HER FAMILY.

WWW.FRANCESCASIMON.COM WWW.HORRIDHENRY.CO.UK @SIMON_FRANCESCA

TONY ROSS

TONY ROSS WAS BORN IN LONDON AND STUDIED AT THE LIVERPOOL SCHOOL OF ART AND DESIGN. HE HAS WORKED AS A CARTOONIST, A GRAPHIC DESIGNER, AN ADVERTISING ART DIRECTOR AND A UNIVERSITY LECTURER.

TONY IS ONE OF THE MOST POPULAR AND SUCCESSFUL CHILDREN'S ILLUSTRATORS OF ALL TIME, BEST KNOWN FOR ILLUSTRATING HORRID HENRY AND THE WORKS OF DAVID WALLIAMS, AS WELL AS HIS OWN HUGELY POPULAR SERIES, THE LITTLE PRINCESS. HE LIVES IN MACCLESFIELD.

HORRID HENRY

FRIGHT NIGHT

FRANCESCA SIMON

ILLUSTRATED BY TONY ROSS

Orion

ORION CHILDREN'S BOOKS

Stories originally published in "Horrid Henry and the Haunted House", "Horrid Henry and the Bogey Babysitter", "Horrid Henry and the Zombie Vampire", "Horrid Henry's Monster Movie"and "Horrid Henry and the Cannibal Curse" respectively.

This collection first published in Great Britain in 2020 by Hodder and Stoughton

1 3 5 7 9 10 8 6 4 2

Text © Francesca Simon, 1999, 2002, 2011, 2012, 2015
Illustrations © Tony Ross, 1999, 2002, 2011, 2012, 2015
Puzzles and activities © Orion Children's Books, 2020
Additional images © Shutterstock

A CIP catalogue record for this book is available from the British Library.

ISBN 978 1 5101 0718 2

Printed and bound in Great Britain by Clays Ltd, Elcograf S.p.A.

The paper and board used in this book are from well-managed forests and other responsible sources.

MIX
Paper from
responsible sources
FSC® C104740

Orion Children's Books
An imprint of
Hachette Children's Group
Part of Hodder and Stoughton
Carmelite House
50 Victoria Embankment
London EC4Y 0DZ

An Hachette UK Company
www.hachette.co.uk

www.hachettechildrens.co.uk
www.horridhenry.co.uk

CONTENTS

STORY 1

HORRID HENRY HAUNTED HOUSE

 9

STORY 2

HORRID HENRY TRICKS AND TREATS

 41

STORY 3

HORRID HENRY AND THE MAD PROFESSOR

 73

STORY 4

HORRID HENRY MONSTER MOVIE

 103

STORY 5

HORRID HENRY'S HORRID WEEKEND

 137

STORY 6

HORRID HENRY'S BAD BOOK

175

HORRID HENRY

HAUNTED HOUSE

"NO WAY!" shrieked Horrid Henry.

He was not staying the weekend with his **slimy** cousin Stuck-Up Steve, and that was that. He sat in the back seat of the car with his arms folded.

"Yes you are," said Mum.

"Steve can't wait to see you," said Dad.

This was not exactly true. After Henry had sprayed Steve with GREEN GOO last Christmas, *and* helped himself to a few of Steve's presents, Steve had **sworn revenge**.

Under the circumstances, Henry
thought it would be a good idea to
keep out of Steve's way.

And now Mum had arranged for
him to spend the weekend while she
and Dad went off on their own! Perfect
Peter was staying with Tidy Ted, and
he was stuck with Steve.

"It's a great chance for you boys to
become good friends," she said. "Steve
is a very nice boy."

"I feel sick," said Henry, coughing.

"Stop faking," said Mum. "You
were well enough to play football

all morning."

"I'm too tired," said Henry, yawning.

"I'm sure you'll get plenty of rest at
Aunt Ruby's," said Dad firmly.

"**I'M NOT GOING!**" howled
Henry.

Mum and Dad took Henry by the
arms, DRAGGED him to Rich Aunt Ruby's
door, and rang the bell.

The massive door opened
immediately.

"Welcome, Henry," said Rich Aunt
Ruby, giving him a great smacking kiss.

"Henry, how lovely to see you," said

Stuck-up Steve sweetly. "That's a very nice second-hand jumper you're wearing."

"Hush, Steve," said Rich Aunt Ruby. "I think Henry looks very smart."

Henry glared at Steve. Thank goodness he'd remembered his Goo-Shooter. He had a feeling he might need it.

"Goodbye, Henry," said Mum. "Be good. Ruby, thank you so much for having him."

"Our pleasure," lied Aunt Ruby.

The great door closed.

Henry was alone in the house with his **ARCH-ENEMY**.

Henry looked **GRIMLY** at Steve.

What a **horrible** boy, he thought.

Steve looked **GRIMLY** at Henry.

What a **horrible** boy, he thought.

"Why don't you both go upstairs and play in Steve's room till supper's ready?" said Aunt Ruby.

"I'll show Henry where he's sleeping first," said Steve.

"Good idea," said Aunt Ruby.

Reluctantly, Henry followed his cousin up the wide staircase.

"I bet you're SCARED of the dark," said Steve.

"Course I'm not," said Henry.

"That's good," said Steve. "This is my room," he added, opening the door to an ENORMOUS bedroom.

Horrid Henry stared longingly at the shelves filled to BURSTING with zillions of toys and games.

"Of course all *my* toys are brand new. **DON'T YOU DARE TOUCH ANYTHING**," hissed Steve. "They're all mine and only *I* can play with them."

Henry **SCOWLED**. When he was king he'd use Steve's head for target practice.

They continued all the way to the top. Goodness, this old house was big, thought Henry.

Steve opened the door to a large attic bedroom, with brand-new pink and blue flowered wallpaper, a four-poster bed, an enormous polished wood wardrobe and two large windows.

"You're in the haunted room," said Steve casually.

"**GREAT!**" said Henry. "**I LOVE GHOSTS**."

It would take more than a silly ghost to frighten *him*.

"Don't believe me if you don't want to," said Steve. "Just don't blame me when the ghost starts *wailing*."

"You're nothing but a **BIG fat LIAR**," said Henry. He was sure Steve was lying. He was absolutely sure Steve was lying. He was **ONE MILLION PER CENT** sure that Steve was lying.

He's just trying to pay me back for Christmas, thought Henry.

Steve shrugged. "Suit yourself. See

that stain on the carpet?"

Henry looked down at something brownish.

"That's where the ghost **VAPORISED**," whispered Steve. "Of course, if you're too SCARED to sleep here . . ."

Henry would rather have walked on **HOT COALS** than admit being scared to Steve.

He yawned, as if he'd never heard anything so boring.

"I'm looking forward to meeting the ghost," said Henry.

"Good," said Steve.

"Supper, boys!" called Aunt Ruby.

Henry lay in bed. Somehow he'd survived the **DREADFUL** meal and Stuck-up Steve's bragging about his expensive *clothes*, **TOYS** and *trainers*. Now here he was, alone in the attic at the top of the house. He'd jumped into bed, carefully avoiding the faded brown patch on the floor. He was sure it was just spilled **COLA** or something, but just in case . . .

Henry looked around him. The only

thing he didn't like was the huge wardrobe opposite the bed. It *loomed* up in the darkness at him. You could hide a body in that wardrobe, thought Henry, then rather wished he hadn't.

"**OOOOOOOOOH**."

Henry stiffened.

Had he just imagined the sound of someone moaning?

Silence.

Nothing, thought Henry, snuggling down under the covers. Just the wind.

"**OOOOOOOOOH**."

This time the moaning was a fraction louder. The HAIRS on Henry's neck stood up. He gripped the sheets tightly.

"**HAAAAAAHHHHHHH**."

Henry sat up.

"HAAAAAAAAAAHHHHHHHHHHHH."

The ghostly breathy moaning sound was not coming from **OUTSIDE**. It appeared to be coming from **INSIDE** the giant wardrobe.

Quickly, Henry switched on the bedside light.

What am I going to do? thought Henry. He wanted to run *screaming* to his aunt.

But the truth was, Henry was too frightened to move.

Some **DREADFUL MOANING THING** was inside the wardrobe.

Just waiting to get *him*.

And then Horrid Henry
remembered who he was.
LEADER OF A PIRATE GANG.
Afraid of nothing
(except injections).

I'll just get up and
check inside that
wardrobe, he thought.
Am I a man or a mouse?

MOUSE! he thought.

He did not move.

"OOOOOOOOOAAAAAHHHHHH,"
moaned the **THING**. The unearthly

noises were getting louder.

Shall I wait here for **IT** to get me, or shall I make a move first? thought Henry. Silently, he reached under the bed for his GOO-SHOOTER.

Then slowly, he swung his feet over the bed.

Tiptoe. Tiptoe. Tiptoe.

Holding his breath, Horrid Henry stood outside the wardrobe.

"HAHAHAHAHAHAHAHAHAHAHA!"

Henry jumped. Then he flung open the door and fired.

SPLAT!

"HAHAHAHAHAHAHAHAHA
HAHAHAUGHHH—"

The wardrobe was empty.

Except for something small and greeny-black on the top shelf.

It looked like — it was!

Henry reached up and took it.

It was a cassette player. Covered in **green goo**.

Inside was a tape. It was called **"Dr Jekyll's Spooky Sounds."**

Steve, thought Horrid Henry

grimly. **REVENGE!**

"Did you sleep well, dear?" asked
Aunt Ruby at breakfast.

"Like a log," said Henry.

"No **STRANGE** noises?" asked
Steve.

"No," smiled Henry *sweetly*. "Why, did
you hear something?"

Steve looked disappointed. Horrid
Henry kept his face blank. He
couldn't wait for the evening.

Horrid Henry had a busy day.

He went ice-skating.

He went to the cinema.

He played football.

After supper, Henry went straight
to bed.

"It's been a **LOVELY** day," he
said. "But I'm tired. Goodnight, Aunt
Ruby. Goodnight, Steve."

"Goodnight, Henry," said Ruby.
Steve **IGNORED** him.

But Henry did not go to his
bedroom. Instead he **sneaked** into
Steve's.

He **WRIGGLED** under Steve's bed
and lay there, waiting.

Soon Steve came into the room.
Henry resisted the urge to reach out

and seize Steve's SKINNY leg. He had
something much SCARIER in mind.

He heard Steve putting on his blue
bunny pyjamas and jumping into bed.
Henry waited until the room was
dark.

Steve lay above him, humming to
himself.

"Dooby dooby dooby do," sang Steve.

Slowly, Henry reached up, and ever
so slightly, poked the mattress.

Silence.

"Dooby dooby dooby do," sang Steve, a
little more quietly.

Henry reached up and poked the
mattress again.

Steve sat up.

Then he lay back.

Henry poked the mattress again,
ever so slightly.

"Must be my imagination,"
muttered Steve.

Henry allowed several moments to
pass. Then he TWITCHED the duvet.

"Mummy," whimpered Steve.

Jab! Henry gave the mattress a
definite poke.

"AHHHHHHHHHHHHH!"

screamed Steve. He leapt up and
ran out of the room. **"MUMMY! HELP!
MONSTERS!"**

Henry scrambled out of the room

and ran silently up to his attic.
Quick as he could he put on his
pyjamas, then clattered noisily back
down the stairs to Steve's room.

Aunt Ruby was on her hands and
knees, peering under the bed. Steve
was shivering and quivering in the
corner.

"There's nothing here, Steve," she
said firmly.

"What's wrong?" asked Henry.

"Nothing," muttered Steve.

"You're not scared of the dark, are
you?" said Henry.

33

"Back to bed, boys," said Aunt
Ruby. She left the room.

**"AHHHHH, MUMMY, HELP!
MONSTERS!"** mimicked Henry,
sticking out his tongue.

"MUM!" wailed Steve. "Henry's
being horrid!"

"GO TO BED, BOTH OF YOU!"
shrieked Ruby.

"Watch out for monsters," said
Henry.

Steve did not move from his corner.

"Want to swap rooms tonight?" said
Henry.

Steve did not wait to be asked twice.

"Oh yes," said Steve.

"Go on up," said Henry. "Sweet dreams."

Steve *dashed* out of his bedroom as fast as he could.

Tee hee, thought Horrid Henry, pulling Steve's toys down from the shelves. Now, what would he play with first?

Oh, yes. He'd left a few spooky sounds of his own under the attic bed - just in case.

HORRID HENRY
TRICKS AND TREATS

Hallowe'en! Oh happy, happy day! Every year Horrid Henry could not believe it: an entire day devoted to stuffing your face with *sweets* and playing **HORRID TRICKS**. Best of all, you were *supposed* to stuff your face and play **HORRID TRICKS**. Whoopee!

Horrid Henry was armed and ready. He had *loo roll*. He had **water pistols**. He had SHAVING FOAM. Oh my, would he be playing tricks tonight. Anyone who didn't instantly hand over a fistful of *sweets* would

41

get it with the foam. And woe betide any fool who gave him an apple. Horrid Henry knew how to treat rotten grown-ups like that.

His red and black devil costume lay ready on the bed, complete with EVIL mask, twinkling horns, trident and whippy tail. He'd scare everyone wearing that.

"Heh heh heh," said Horrid Henry, practising his evil laugh.

"Henry," came a little voice outside his bedroom door, "come and see my new costume."

"No," said Henry.

"Oh PLEASE, Henry," said his younger brother, Perfect Peter.

"No," said Henry. "I'm busy."

"You're just jealous because *my* costume is nicer than yours," said Peter.

"Am not."

"Are too."

Come to think of it, what *was* Peter wearing? Last year he'd copied Henry's **MONSTER** costume and ruined Henry's Hallowe'en. What if he were copying Henry's **devil** costume? That would be just like that **HORRIBLE**

little copycat.

"All right, you can come in for two seconds," said Henry.

A **BIG**, pink bouncy bunny bounded into Henry's room. It had little white bunny ears. It had a little white bunny tail. It had pink polka dots everywhere else. Horrid Henry groaned. What a stupid costume. Thank goodness *he* wasn't wearing it.

"Isn't it great?" said Perfect Peter.

"**NO**," said Henry. "**It's horrible.**"

"You're just saying that to be mean, Henry," said Peter, bouncing up and down. "I can't wait to go trick-or-treating in it tonight."

Oh no. **Horrid Henry** felt as if he'd been **PUNCHED** in the stomach. Henry would be expected to go out trick-or-treating — with Peter! He, Henry, would have to walk around with a pink polka dot bunny. Everyone would see him. The shame of it! Rude Ralph would never stop teasing him. Moody Margaret would call him a bunny

wunny. How could he
play tricks on people with a
pink polka dot bunny following him
everywhere? He was ruined. His name
would be a joke.

"YOU CAN'T WEAR THAT," said Henry
desperately.

"Yes I can," said Peter.

"I won't let you," said Henry.

Perfect Peter looked at Henry. "You're
just jealous."

Grrr! Horrid Henry was about to
tear that **stupid** costume off Peter

when, suddenly, he had an idea.

It was painful.

It was HUMILIATING.

But anything was better than having Peter prancing about in pink polka dots.

"Tell you what," said Henry, "just because I'm so nice I'll let you borrow my **MONSTER** costume. You've always wanted to wear it."

"**NO!**" said Peter. "I want to be a bunny."

"But you're supposed to be **SCARY** for Hallowe'en," said Henry.

"I am **SCARY**," said Peter. "I'm going to **bounce** up to people and yell '**BOO**'."

"I can make you **REALLY SCARY**, Peter," said Horrid Henry.

"How?" said Peter.

"Sit down and I'll show you." Henry patted his desk chair.

"What are you going to do?" said Peter suspiciously. He took a step back.

"Nothing," said Henry. "I'm just trying to help you."

Perfect Peter didn't move.

"How can I be **SCARIER?**" he
said cautiously.

"I can give you a **SCARY** haircut,"
said Henry.

 Perfect Peter
clutched his curls.

"But I like my
hair," he said
feebly.

"This is Hallowe'en,"
said Henry. "Do you want to be
SCARY or don't you?"

"UM, UM, UH," said Peter, as Henry
pushed him down in the chair and

got out the scissors.

"Not too much," squealed Peter.

"Of course not," said Horrid Henry.
"Just sit back and relax, I promise
you'll love this."

Horrid Henry
twirled the
scissors.

SNIP!

SNIP!

SNIP! SNIP!

Magnificent, thought Horrid Henry. He gazed proudly at his work. Maybe he should be a hairdresser when he grew up. Yes! Henry could see it now. Customers would queue for miles for one of *Monsieur Henri's* **SCARY** *snips*. Shame his genius was wasted on someone as yucky as Peter. Still . . .

"You look great, Peter," said Henry. "REALLY SCARY. **ATOMIC BUNNY**. Go and have a look."

Peter went over and looked in the mirror.

"AAAAAAAAAARGGGGGGG!"

"Scared yourself, did you?" said Henry. "That's great."

"AAAAAAAAAARGGGGGGG!" howled Peter.

Mum ran into the room.

"AAAAAAAAAARGGGGGGG!" howled Mum.

"AAAAAAAAAARGGGGGGG!" howled Peter.

"Henry!" screeched Mum. "What have you done! You **horrid, horrid** boy!"

What was left of Peter's hair stuck up in ragged tufts all over his head. On

one side was a
BIG BALD PATCH.

"I was just
making him
look SCARY,"
protested Henry. "He said I could."

"Henry made
me!" said Peter.
"My poor
baby," said Mum.
She glared at
Henry.

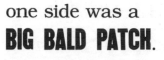

"No trick-or-treating for you,"
said Mum. "You'll stay here."

Horrid Henry could hardly believe his ears. This was the **WORST** thing that had ever happened to him.

"**NO!**" howled Henry. This was all Peter's fault.

"I hate you, Peter!" he screeched. Then he **attacked**. He was Medusa, *coiling* round her victim with her snaky hair.

"Aaaahh!" screeched Peter.

"**HENRY!**" shouted Mum. "Go to your room!"

Mum and Peter left the house to go trick-or-treating. Henry had **SCREAMED** and **sobbed** and BEGGED. He'd put on his devil costume, just in case his tears melted their stony hearts. But no. His MEAN, **horrible** parents wouldn't change their mind. Well, they'd be sorry. They'd all be sorry.

Dad came into the sitting room. He was holding a large shopping bag.

"Henry, I've got some work to finish so I'm going to let you hand out treats to any trick-or-treaters."

Horrid Henry stopped plotting his

revenge. Had Dad gone mad? Hand
out 𝓉𝓇𝑒𝒶𝓉𝓈? What kind of
punishment was
this?

**Horrid
Henry** fought
to keep a **BIG**
smile off
his face.
"Here's the
Hallowe'en stuff,
Henry," said Dad. He handed Henry the
heavy bag. "But remember," he added
sternly, "these 𝓉𝓇𝑒𝒶𝓉𝓈 are not for you:

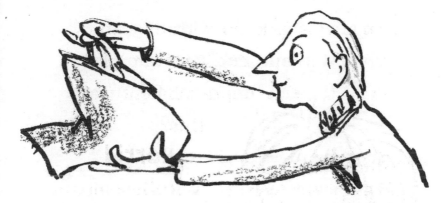

they're to give away."

Yeah, right, thought Henry.

"OK, DAD," he said as meekly as he could. "Whatever you say."

Dad went back to the kitchen. Now was his chance! **Horrid Henry** *leapt* on the bag. Wow, was it full! He'd **GRAB** all the good stuff, throw

back anything yucky with lime or
peppermint, and he'd have enough
sweets to keep him going for at least
a week!

Henry yanked open the bag. A
terrible sight met his eyes. The bag
was full of satsumas. And apples. And
walnuts in their shells. No wonder his
horrible parents had trusted him to
be in charge of it.

DING DONG.

Slowly, Horrid Henry **HEAVED** his
HEAVY bones to the door. There was
his empty, useless trick-or-treat bag,

sitting forlornly by the entrance. Henry gave it a kick, then opened the door and glared.

"**whaddya want?**" snapped Horrid Henry.

"**Trick-or-treat,**" whispered Weepy William. He was dressed as a pirate.

Horrid Henry held out the bag of **horrors.** "Lucky dip!" he announced.

"Close your eyes for a big surprise!"

William certainly would be surprised at what a **ROTTEN** treat he'd be getting.

Weepy William put down his swag bag, closed his eyes tight, then *plunged* his hand into Henry's lucky dip. He rummaged and he rummaged and he rummaged, hoping to find something better than satsumas.

Horrid Henry eyed Weepy William's **bulging** swag bag.

Go on, Henry, urged the bag. He'll never notice.

Horrid Henry did not wait to be asked twice.

Dip! Zip! Pop!

Horrid Henry *grabbed* a big handful of William's sweets and popped them inside his empty bag.

Weepy William opened his eyes.

"Did you take some of my sweets?"

"No," said Henry.

William peeked inside his bag and burst into tears.

"Waaaaaaaa!" wailed William.
"Henry took—"

Henry *pushed* him out and **slammed** the door.

Dad came running.

"What's wrong?"

"Nothing," said Henry. "Just William crying 'cause he's scared of pumpkins."

Phew, thought Henry. That was close. Perhaps he had been a little too greedy.

DING DONG.

It was Lazy Linda wearing a

pillowcase
over her head.
Gorgeous
Gurinder was
with her, dressed
as a scarecrow.

"Trick-or-treat!"
"Trick-or-treat!"

"Close your eyes for a **BIG** surprise!"
said Henry, holding out the lucky dip
bag.

"OOH, A LUCKY DIP!" squealed Linda.

Lazy Linda and Gorgeous Gurinder
put down their bags, closed their eyes

and reached into
the lucky dip.

Dip! **Zip!** **Pop!** **Dip!** **Zip!** **Pop!**

Lazy Linda opened her eyes.

"You give the **WORST** treats ever,
Henry," said Linda, gazing at her
walnut in disgust.

"We won't be coming back *here*,"
sniffed Gorgeous Gurinder.

Tee hee, thought Horrid Henry.

DING DONG.

It was Beefy Bert. He was wearing a robot costume.

"Hi, Bert, got any good *sweets?*" asked Henry.

"I dunno," said Beefy Bert.

Horrid Henry soon found out that he did. **Lots** and **lots** and **lots** of them. So did Moody Margaret, Sour

Susan, Jolly Josh and Tidy Ted. Soon
Henry's bag was stuffed with treats.

DING DONG.

Horrid Henry opened the door.

"BOO," said Atomic Bunny.

Henry's sweet bag! Help! Mum
would see it!

"EEEEEK!" screeched
Horrid Henry. "Help!
Save me!"

Quickly, he ran
upstairs clutching
his bag and hid
it safely under his

bed. Phew, that was close.

"Don't be scared, Henry, it's only me," called Perfect Peter.

Horrid Henry came back downstairs.

"**NO!**" said Henry. "I'd never have known."

"Really?" said Peter.

"Really," said Henry.

"Everyone just gave *sweets* this year," said Perfect Peter. "**YUCK**."

Horrid Henry held out the lucky dip.

"Ooh, a satsuma," said Peter.

"Aren't I lucky!"

"I hope you've learned your lesson, Henry," said Mum sternly.

"I certainly have," said Horrid Henry, eyeing Perfect Peter's bulging bag. "Good things come to those who wait."

HORRID HENRY

AND THE MAD PROFESSOR

Horrid Henry grabbed
the top secret sweet tin
he kept hidden under his
bed. It was jam-packed with all
his favourites: Big Boppers. Nose
Pickers. DIRT BALLS. HOT SNOT.
Gooey Chewies. SCRUNCHY
MUNCHIES.

Yummy!!!

Hmmm boy! Horrid Henry's
mouth watered as he prised off the
lid. Which to have first? A DIRT
BALL? Or a Gooey Chewy? Actually,
he'd just scoff the lot. It had been

ages since he'd . . .

Huh?

Where were all his chocolates?
Where were all his *sweets*? Who'd
nicked them? Had Margaret invaded
his room? Had Peter sneaked in?
How dare— Oh. **Horrid Henry**
suddenly remembered. He'd eaten
them all.

RATS.

RATS.

TRIPLE RATS.

Well, he'd just have to go and buy
more. He was sure to have **LOADS**

of pocket money left.

Chocolate, here I come, thought Horrid Henry, heaving his bones and dashing over to his skeleton bank.

He shook it. Then he shook it again.

There wasn't even a rattle.

How could he have **NO MONEY** and no sweets? It was so unfair! Just last night Peter had been boasting about having £7.48 in his piggy bank. And loads of sweets left over from Hallowe'en. **Horrid Henry** scowled. Why did Peter always have money?

Why did he, Henry, never have money?

Money was totally wasted on Peter. What was the point of Peter having POCKET MONEY since he never spent it? Come to think of it, what was the point of Peter having sweets since he never ate them?

There was a shuffling, scuttling noise, then Perfect Peter dribbled into Henry's bedroom carrying all his soft toys.

"Get out of my room, *worm!*" bellowed Horrid Henry, holding his

nose. "You're stinking it up."

"I am not," said Peter.

"Are too, **SMELLY PANTS**."

"I do not have smelly pants," said
Peter.

"Do too, **woofy, poofy, pongy
pants**."

Peter opened his mouth, then closed it.

"Henry, will you play with me?"
said Peter.

"**NO**."

"Please?"

"No!"

"Pretty please?"

"No!!"

"But we could play school with all my cuddly toys," said Peter. "Or have a tea party with them . . ."

"For the last time, **NOOOOOOO!**" screamed Horrid Henry.

"You never play with me," said Perfect Peter.

"That's 'cause you're a **toad-faced nappy wibble bibble**,"

said Horrid Henry. "Now go away
and leave me alone."

"Mum! Henry's calling me names
again!" screamed Peter. "He called me
wibble bibble."

"Henry! Don't be **HORRID!**"
shouted Mum.

"I'm not being horrid, Peter's
annoying me!" yelled Henry.

"Henry's annoying me!" yelled Peter.
"MAKE HIM STOP!" screamed
Henry and Peter.

Mum ran into the room.

"Boys. If you can't play nicely then

leave each other alone," said Mum.

"Henry won't play with me," wailed
Peter. "He never plays with me."

"Henry! Why can't you play with
your brother?" said Mum. "When
I was little, Ruby and I played
beautifully together all the time."

Horrid Henry **SCOWLED**.

"Because he's a **wormy worm**," said Henry.

"Mum! Henry just called me a wormy worm," wailed Peter.

"Don't call your brother names," said Mum.

"Peter only wants to play **stupid** baby games," said Henry.

"I do not," said Peter.

"If you're not going to play together then you can do your chores," said Mum.

"I've done mine," said Peter. "I fed Fluffy, cleaned out the litter tray and tidied my room."

Mum beamed. "Peter, you are the *best boy in the world.*"

Horrid Henry scowled. He'd been far too busy reading his **COMICS** to empty the wastepaper bins and tidy his room. He stuck out his tongue at Peter behind Mum's back.

"Henry's making **HORRIBLE** faces at me," said Peter.

"Henry, please be nice for once and play with Peter," said Mum. She sighed and left the room.

Henry *glared* at Peter.

Peter *glared* at Henry.

Horrid Henry was about to push
Peter out the door when suddenly
he had a brilliant, SPECTACULAR
idea. It was so brilliant and so
SPECTACULAR that Horrid
Henry couldn't believe he was still
standing in his bedroom and hadn't
BLASTED off into outer space
trailing clouds of glory. Why had
he never thought of this before?
It was **MAGNIFICENT**. It was genius.
One day he would start *Henry's
Genius Shop*, where people would

pay a million pounds to buy his
SUPER FANTASTIC ideas. But until
then . . . "Okay, Peter, I'll play with
you," said Horrid Henry. He smiled
sweetly.

Perfect Peter could hardly believe
his ears.

"You'll . . . play with me?" said
Perfect Peter.

"Sure," said **Horrid Henry**.

"What do you want to play?" asked
Peter cautiously. The last time Peter
could remember Henry playing with
him they'd played **Cannibals and**

Dinner. Peter had had to be dinner . . .

"Let's play **Robot and Mad Professor**," said Henry.

"Okay," said Perfect Peter. Wow. That sounded a lot more exciting than his usual favourite game — writing lists of **vegetables** or having *ladybird tea parties* with his stuffed toys. He'd probably have to be the robot, and do what Henry said, but it would be worth it, to play such a fun game.

"I'll be the robot," said Horrid Henry.

Peter's jaw dropped.

"Go on," said Henry. "You're the mad

professor. Tell me
what to do."

WOW. Henry was even letting him
be the *mad professor*. Maybe he'd
been wrong about Henry . . . maybe
Henry had been struck by lightning
and changed into a nice brother . . .

"Robot," ordered Perfect Peter.
"March around the room."

Horrid Henry didn't budge.

"Robot!" said Peter. "I order you to
march."

"Pro—fes—sor! I—need—twenty-
five—p—to—move," said Henry in a

robotic voice. "Twenty-five p. Twenty-five p. Twenty-five p."

"Twenty-five p?" said Peter.

"That's the rules of **Robot and Mad Professor**," said Henry, shrugging.

"Okay, Henry," said Peter, rummaging in his bank. He handed Henry 25p.

Yes! thought **Horrid Henry**.

Horrid Henry took a few stiff steps, then slowed down and stopped.

"More," said robotic Henry. "More. My batteries have run

down. More."

Perfect Peter handed over another 25p.

Henry *lurched* around for a few more steps, **crashed** into the wall and collapsed on the floor.

"I need sweets to get up," said the robot. "Fetch me sweets. Systems overload. Sweets. Sweets. Sweets."

Perfect Peter dropped two sweets into Henry's hand. Henry twitched his foot.

"More," said the robot. "Lots more."

Perfect Peter dropped four more

sweets. Henry jerked up into a sitting position.

"I will now tell you my top secret—secret—secret—secret—" stuttered **Horrid Henry**. "Cross—my—palm—with—silver and sweets . . ." He held out his robot hand. Peter filled it.

TEE HEE.

"I want to be the robot now," said Peter.

"Okay, robot," said Henry. "Run upstairs and empty all the waste-paper baskets. Bet you can't do it in thirty seconds."

"Yes I can," said Peter.

"Nah, you're too **rusty** and PUNY," said Horrid Henry.

"Am not," said Peter.

"Then prove it, robot," said Henry.

"But aren't you going to give me—" faltered Peter.

"**MOVE!**" bellowed Henry. "They

don't call me the **MAD** professor for nothing!!!"

Playing **Robot and Mad Professor** was a bit less fun than Peter had anticipated. Somehow, his piggy bank was now empty and Henry's skeleton bank was full. And somehow most of Peter's Hallowe'en sweets were now in Henry's sweet box.

Robot and Mad Professor was the most **FUN** Henry had ever had playing with Peter. Now that he

had all Peter's money and all Peter's
sweets, could he trick Peter into doing
all his chores as well?

"Let's play school," said Peter. That
would be safe. There was no way
Henry could trick him playing that . . .

"I've got a better idea," said Henry.
"Let's play SLAVES AND MASTERS. You're the
slave. I order you to . . ."

"No," interrupted Peter. "I don't want
to." Henry couldn't make him.

"Okay," said Henry. "We can play
school. You can be the tidy monitor."

Oh! Peter loved being tidy monitor.

"We're going to play Clean Up the Classroom!" said Henry. "The classroom is in here. So, get to work."

Peter looked around at the great mess of TOYS and DIRTY CLOTHES and COMICS and empty wrappers scattered all over Henry's room.

"I thought we'd start by taking the register," said Peter.

"Nah," said Henry. "That's the baby way to play school. You have to start by tidying the classroom. You're the tidy monitor."

"What are you?" said Peter.

"The teacher, of course," said Henry.

"Can I be the teacher next?" said Peter.

"Sure," said Henry. "We'll swap after you finish your job."

Henry lay on his bed and read his COMIC and stuffed the rest of Peter's sweets into his mouth. Peter tidied.

Ah, this was the life.

"It's very quiet in here," said Mum, popping her head round the door. "What's going on?"

"Nothing," said Horrid Henry.

"Why is Peter tidying your room?" said Mum.

"Cause he's the tidy monitor," said Henry.

Perfect Peter burst into tears. "Henry's taken all my money and all my sweets and made me do all his chores," he wailed.

HENRY!" shouted Mum. "**YOU HORRID BOY!**"

On the bad side, Mum made Henry give Peter back all his money. But on the good side, all his chores were done for the week. And he couldn't give Peter back his sweets because he'd eaten them all.

Result!

HORRID HENRY

MONSTER MOVIE

Horrid Henry loved scary movies. He loved nothing more than curling up on the comfy **BLACK** chair with a huge bag of popcorn and a **FIZZYWIZZ** drink, and jumping out of his seat in shock every few minutes. He loved *wailing ghosts,* **oozing swamps** and **BLOODTHIRSTY MONSTERS**. No film was too scary or too creepy for **Horrid Henry**. **MWAHAHAHAHAHAHA!**

Perfect Peter hated scary movies. He hated nothing more than hiding behind the comfy **BLACK** chair, covering

his eyes and jumping out of his skin
in shock every few seconds. He hated
ghosts and **swamps** and **MONSTERS**.
Even Santa Claus saying "**HO HO HO**" too
loudly scared him.

Thanks to Peter being the biggest
SCAREDY-CAT who ever lived,
Mum and Dad would never take Henry
to see any scary films.

And now, the scariest, most
frightening, most **TERRIBLE** film
ever was in town. **Horrid Henry** was
desperate to see it.

"You're not seeing that film and that's

final," said Mum.

"Absolutely no way," said Dad. "Far too scary."

"But I love *scary* movies!" shrieked Horrid Henry.

"I don't," said Mum.

"I don't," said Dad.

"I hate scary movies," said Perfect Peter. "Please can we see *The Big Bunny Caper* instead?"

"**NO!**" shrieked Horrid Henry.

"Stop shouting, Henry," said Mum.

"But everyone's seen **The Vampire Zombie Werewolf**," moaned Horrid Henry. "Everyone but me."

MOODY MARGARET had seen it, and said it was the best **HORROR** film ever.

Fiery Fiona had seen it three times. "And I'm seeing it three more times," she squealed.

Rude Ralph said he'd run **SCREAMING** from the cinema.

AAAARRRRGGGGGHHHHHH!

Horrid Henry thought he would explode, he wanted to see **The Vampire Zombie Werewolf** so much. But no. The film came and went, and Horrid Henry **wailed** and **gnashed**.

So he couldn't believe his luck when Rude Ralph came up to him one day at playtime and said:

"I've got **The Vampire Zombie Werewolf** film on DVD. Want to come over and watch it after school?"

Did he ever!

Horrid Henry squeezed onto the sofa between Rude Ralph and Brainy Brian. Dizzy Dave sat on the floor next to Jolly Josh and Aerobic Al. Anxious Andrew sat on a chair. He'd already covered his face with his hands. Even **MOODY MARGARET** and Sour Susan were there, squabbling over who got to sit in the armchair and who had to sit on the floor.

"Okay everyone, this is it," said Rude Ralph. "The **SCARIEST** film ever. Are we ready?"

"Yeah!"

Horrid Henry gripped the sofa as the eerie piano music started.

There was a **DEEP, DARK FOREST**.

"I'm scared!" wailed Anxious Andrew.

"Nothing's happened yet," said Horrid Henry.

A boy and a girl ran through the **SHIVERY**, shadowy trees.

"Is it safe to look?" gasped Anxious Andrew.

"Shhh," said Moody Margaret.

"You shhh!" said Horrid Henry.

"MWAHAAAAHAAAAHAHAHAA!" bellowed Dizzy Dave.

"I M SCARED!" shrieked Anxious Andrew.

"Shut up!" shouted Rude Ralph.

The pale girl stopped running and turned to the bandaged boy.

"I can't kiss you or I'll turn into a zombie," sulked the girl.

"I can't kiss you or I'll turn into a

vampire," scowled the boy.

"But our love is so strong!" wailed the vampire girl and the zombie boy.

"Not as strong as me!" howled the werewolf, leaping out from behind a tree stump.

"**AAAAAAAARRRRGGGHHH!**" screeched Anxious Andrew.

"**SHUT UP!**" shouted Henry and Ralph.

"Leave her alone, you walking bandage," said the werewolf.

"Leave him alone, you smelly fur ball," said the vampire.

"This isn't **SCARY**," said Horrid
Henry.

"Shh," said Margaret.

"Go away!" shouted the zombie.

"You go away, you **big meanie**,"
snarled the werewolf.

"Don't you know that two's company
and three's a crowd?" hissed the
vampire.

"I challenge you both to an arm-
wrestling contest," howled the werewolf.
"The winner gets to keep the arms."

"Or in your case the paws," sniffed
the vampire.

"This is the **WORST** film I've ever seen," said Horrid Henry.

"**Shut up, Henry**," said Margaret.

"We're trying to watch," said Susan.

"Ralph, I thought you said this was a really **SCARY** film," hissed Henry. "Have you actually seen it before?"

Rude Ralph looked at the floor.

"No," admitted Ralph. "But everyone said they'd seen it and I didn't want to be left out."

"Margaret's a big fat liar too," said Susan. "She never saw it either."

"Shut up, Susan!" shrieked Margaret.

"**AWHOOOOOOO**," howled the werewolf.

Horrid Henry was disgusted. He could make a much scarier film. In fact . . . what was stopping him? Who better to make the **SCARIEST** film of all time than Henry? How hard could it be to make a film? You just pointed a camera and yelled, "Action!" Then he'd be **RICH RICH RICH**. He'd need a spare house just to stash all his cash. And he'd be famous, too. Everyone would be begging for a role in one of his mega-horror blockbusters. Please can we be in your new **monster** film? Mum and Dad and Peter would beg. Well, they could beg as long as they liked. He'd give them his *autograph*, but that would be it.

Henry could see the poster now:

HENRY PRODUCTIONS PRESENT:

THE UNDEAD
DEMON MONSTER
WHO WOULD
NOT DIE

STARRING HENRY AS THE MONSTER

WRITTEN AND FILMED AND DIRECTED BY

HENRY

"I could make a really scary film," said Henry.

"Not as scary as the film I could make," said Margaret.

"Ha!" said Henry. "Your **SCARY** film wouldn't scare a toddler."

"Ha!" said Margaret. "Your **SCARY** film would make a baby laugh."

"Oh yeah?" said Henry.

"Yeah," said Margaret.

"Well, we'll just see about that," said Henry.

Horrid Henry walked around his garden, clutching Mum's camcorder.

He could turn the garden into a **SWAMP** . . . flood a few flower

beds . . . rip up the lawn and throw buckets of **mud** at the windows as the monster squelched his monstrous way through the undergrowth, growling and devouring, biting and—

"Henry, can I be in your movie?" said Peter.

"No," said Henry. "I'm making a scary monster film. No nappy babies."

"I am not a nappy baby," said Peter.

"Are too."

"Am not. Mum! Henry won't let me be in his film."

"**HENRY!**" yelled Mum. "Let Peter be in your film or you can't borrow the camcorder."

GAH! Why did everyone always get in his way? How could Henry be a great director if other people told him who to put in his film?

"Okay, Peter," said Henry, scowling. "You can be Best Boy."

Best Boy! That sounded super. Wow.

That was a lot better than Peter had
hoped.

"**Best Boy!**" shouted Horrid Henry.
"Get the snack table ready."

"Snack table?" said Peter.

"Setting up the snack table is the
most important part of making a
movie," said Henry. "So I want biscuits
and crisps and **FIZZYWIZZ** drinks —
NOW!" he bellowed. "It's hungry work
making a film."

Film-making next door at Moody Margaret's house was also proceeding slowly.

"How come I have to move the furniture?" said Susan. "You said I could be in your movie."

"Because I'm the director," said Margaret. "So I decide."

"Margaret, you can be the **MONSTER** in my film. No need for any make-up," shouted Horrid Henry over the wall.

"**Shut up, Henry**," said Margaret.

"Susan. Start walking down the path."

"**BOOOOOOOOOOOO**," shouted
Horrid Henry. "**BOOOOOOOOOOOO**."

"Cut!" yelled Margaret. "Quiet!" she
screamed. "I'm making a movie here."

"Peter, hold the torch and shine the
spotlight on me," ordered Henry.

"Hold the torch?" said Peter.

"It's very important," said Henry.

"Mum said you had to let me be in
your movie," said Peter. "Or I'm telling
on you."

Horrid Henry *glared* at Perfect
Peter.

Perfect Peter *glared* at Horrid Henry.

"Mum!" screamed Peter.

"Okay, you can be in the movie,"
said Henry.

"Stop being **HORRID**, Henry,"
shouted Mum. "Or you hand back
that camera instantly."

"I'm not being horrid; that's in the
movie," lied Henry.

Perfect Peter opened his mouth and
then closed it.

"So what's my part?" said Peter.

Perfect Peter stood on the bench in the front garden.

"Now say your line, 'I am too **horrible** to live', and jump off the bench into the crocodile-filled moat, where you are eaten alive and drown," said Henry.

"I don't want to say that," said Peter.

Horrid Henry lowered the camera. "Do you want to be in the film or

don't you?" he hissed.

"I AM TOO HORRIBLE TO LIVE," muttered Peter.

"Louder!" said Henry.

"I AM TOO HORRIBLE TO LIVE," said Peter, a fraction louder.

"And as you drown, **scream** out, 'and I have *smelly pants*'," said Henry.

"What?" said Peter.

TEE HEE, thought **Horrid Henry**.

"But how come you get to play all the other parts, and dance, and sing, and all I get to do is walk about going

WOOOOOOO?" said Susan sourly in next door's garden.

"Because it's my movie," said Margaret.

"Keep it down, we're filming here," said Henry. "Now, Peter, you are walking down the garden path out into the street—"

"I thought I'd just drowned," said Peter.

Henry *rolled* his eyes.

"No, dummy, this is a **HORROR** film. You rose from the dead, and now you're walking down the path singing this song, just before the **HAIRY SCARY MONSTER** leaps out of the bushes and rips you to shreds.

"Wibble bibble dribble pants

Bibble baby wibble pants

Wibble pants wibble pants

Dribble dribble dribble pants,"

sang Horrid Henry.

Perfect Peter hesitated. "But Henry, why would my character sing that song?"

Henry *glared* at Peter.

"Because I'm the director and I say so," said Henry.

Perfect Peter's lip trembled. He started walking.

"Wibble bibble dribble pants

Bibble baby wibble pants

Wibble pants—"

"I don't want to!" came a screech from next door's front garden.

"Susan, you have to be covered up in a sheet," said Margaret.

"But no one will see my face and know it's me," said Susan.

"Duh," said Margaret. "You're playing a ghost."

Sour Susan *flung* off the sheet.

"Well, I quit," said Susan.

"You're fired!" shouted Margaret.

"I don't want to sing that dribble pants song," said Peter.

"Then you're fired!" screamed Henry.

"No!" screamed Perfect Peter. "I quit."

And he ran out of the front garden gate, **SHRIEKING** and *wailing*.

Wow, thought Horrid Henry. He chased after Peter, filming.

"I've had it!" screamed Sour Susan. "I don't want to be in your stupid film!" She ran off down the road, **SHRIEKING** and *wailing*.

Margaret chased after her, filming.

Cool, thought Horrid Henry, what a perfect end for his film, the puny wimp running off terrified—

BUMP!

Susan and Peter collided and sprawled flat on the pavement.

CRASH!

Henry and Margaret tripped over the screaming Peter and Susan.

SMASH!

Horrid Henry dropped his camcorder.

SMASH!

 dropped her camcorder.

OOPS.

Horrid Henry stared down at the twisted, broken metal as his monster movie lay shattered on the concrete path.

WHOOPS.

Moody Margaret stared down at the cracked camcorder as her Hollywood horror film lay in pieces on the ground.

"Henry!" hissed Margaret.

"Margaret!" hissed Henry.

"This is all your fault!" they wailed.

HORRID HENRY'S

HORRID WEEKEND

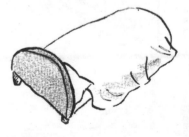

"**NOOOOOOOOO!**" screamed Horrid Henry. "I don't want to spend the weekend with Steve."

"Don't be **HORRID**, Henry," said Mum. "It's very kind of Aunt Ruby to invite us down for the weekend."

"But I **HATE** Aunt Ruby!" shrieked Henry. "And I hate Steve and I hate you!"

"I can't wait to go," said Perfect Peter.

"**Shut up, Peter!**" howled Henry.

"Don't tell your brother to shut up," shouted Mum.

"SHUT UP! SHUT UP! SHUT UP!" And **Horrid**

Henry fell to the floor wailing and screaming and kicking.

STUCK-UP STEVE was Horrid Henry's hideous cousin. Steve hated Henry. Henry hated him. The last time Henry had seen Steve, Henry had **tricked** him into thinking there was a monster under his bed. Steve had sworn revenge. Then there was the other time at the restaurant when . . . well, **Horrid Henry** thought it would be a good idea to avoid Steve

until his cousin
was grown-up
and in prison
for **CRIMES**
~~**AGAINST HUMANITY**~~.

And now his **MEAN, HORRIBLE**
parents were forcing him to spend a
whole precious weekend with the toadiest,
wormiest, smelliest boy who ever slimed
out of a swamp.

Mum sighed. "We're going and that's
that. Ruby says Steve is having a lovely
friend over so that should be extra fun."

Henry stopped screaming and kicking.

Maybe Steve's friend wouldn't be a stuck-up **MONSTER**. Maybe he'd been forced to waste his weekend with Steve, too. After all, who'd volunteer to spend time with Steve? Maybe together they could squish **STUCK-UP STEVE** once and for all.

DING DONG.

Horrid Henry, Perfect Peter, Mum and Dad stood outside Rich Aunt

Ruby's **ENORMOUS** house on a grey, drizzly day. Steve opened the **massive** front door.

"Oh," he sneered. "It's you."

Steve opened the present Mum had brought. It was a SMALL flashlight. Steve put it down.

"I already have a much better one," he said.

"Oh," said Mum.

Another boy stood beside him. A boy who looked vaguely familiar. A boy . . . **Horrid Henry** gasped. Oh no. It was Bill. *Bossy Bill*. The **HORRIBLE** son of Dad's boss. Henry had once **tricked** Bill into photocopying his bottom. Bill had sworn revenge. **Horrid Henry's** insides turned to jelly. Trust **STUCK-UP STEVE** to be friends with **Bossy Bill**. It was bad enough being trapped in a house with one arch-enemy. Now he was stuck in a house with TWO . . .

Stuck-up Steve **SCOWLED** at Henry. "You're wearing that old shirt of mine," he said. "Don't your parents ever buy you new clothes?"

Bossy Bill snorted.

"Steve," said Aunt Ruby. "Don't be rude."

"I wasn't," said Steve. "I was just asking. No harm in asking, is there?"

"No," said Horrid Henry. He smiled at Steve. "So when will Aunt Ruby buy you a new face?"

"**HENRY**," said Mum. "Don't be rude."

"I was just asking," said Henry. "No harm in asking, is there?" he added, glaring at Steve.

Steve *glared* back.

Aunt Ruby beamed. "Henry, Steve and Bill are taking you to their friend Tim's PAINTBALLING party."

"Won't that be **FUN**," said
Mum.

Peter looked frightened.

"Don't worry, Peter," said Aunt
Ruby, "you can help me plant
seedlings while the older boys are
out."

Peter beamed. "Thank you," he said.
"I don't like **PAINTBALLING**. Too
messy and scary."

Paintballing! **Horrid Henry** loved
paintballing. The chance to **splat**
Steve and Bill with **OOEY GOOEY
GLOBS** of paint . . . hmmm, maybe

the weekend was looking up.

"Great!" said Horrid Henry.

"How nice," said Rich Aunt Ruby,
"you boys already know each other.
Think how much fun you're all going
to have sharing Steve's bedroom
together."

Uh-oh, thought **Horrid Henry**.

"Yeah!" said Stuck-Up Steve. "We're looking forward to sharing a room with Henry." His PIGGY eyes gleamed.

"Yeah!" said Bossy Bill. "I can't wait." His piggy eyes gleamed.

"Yeah," said Horrid Henry. He wouldn't be sleeping a wink.

Horrid Henry looked around the **enormous** high-ceilinged bedroom he'd be sharing with his two **evil** enemies for two very long days and one very long night. There was a bunk-bed, which Steve and Bill had already nabbed, and two single beds. Steve's bedroom shelves were stuffed with **ZILLIONS** of new toys and games, as usual.

Bill and Steve smirked at each other. Henry **SCOWLED** at them. What were they plotting?

"Don't you dare touch my **SUPER-BLOOPER BLASTER**," said Steve.

"Don't you dare touch my **Demon Dagger Sabre**," said Bill.

A Super-Blooper Blaster! A Demon Dagger Sabre! Trust Bill and Steve to have the two best toys in the world . . . **RATS**.

"Don't worry," said Henry. "I don't play with baby toys."

"Oh yeah," said **STUCK-UP STEVE**. "Bet you're too much of a baby to jump off my top bunk on to your bed."

"Am not," said Henry.

"We're not allowed to **jump** on beds," said Perfect Peter.

"We're not allowed," mimicked Steve. "I thought you were too poor to even have beds."

"**Ha ha**," said Henry.

"Chicken. Chicken. Scaredy cat," sneered Bossy Bill.

"Squawk!" said Stuck-Up Steve. "I knew you'd be too scared, chicken."

That did it. No one called **Horrid Henry** chicken and lived. As if he, Henry, **LEADER OF A PIRATE GANG**, would be afraid to jump off a top bunk. Ha.

"Don't do it, Henry," said Perfect Peter.

"Shut up, **worm**," said Henry.

"But it's so high," squealed Peter,

squeezing
his eyes shut.

Horrid Henry
clambered up the ladder and
stepped on to the top bunk.

"It's nothing," he lied. "I've jumped
off **MUCH** higher."

"Well, go on then," said Stuck-Up
Steve.

Boing! Horrid Henry bounced.

Boing! Horrid Henry bounced higher. **WHEE!** This bed was very springy.

"We're waiting, chicken," said Bossy Bill.

BOING! BOING! Horrid Henry bent his knees, then . . . leap! He jumped on to the single bed below.

SMASH!

Horrid Henry crashed to the floor as the bed collapsed beneath him.

Huh? What? How could he have **broken** the bed? He hadn't heard any breaking sounds.

It was as if . . . as if . . .

Mum, Dad and Aunt Ruby ran into the room.

"Henry broke the bed," said Stuck-Up Steve.

"We tried to stop him," said Bossy Bill, "but Henry insisted on jumping."

"But . . . but . . ." said Horrid Henry.

"Henry!" wailed Mum. "You **HORRID** boy."

"How could you be so horrid?" said Dad. "No **POCKET MONEY** for a year. Ruby, I'm so sorry."

Aunt Ruby pursed her lips. "These things happen," she said.

"And no **PAINTBALLING** party for you," said Mum.

What?

"No!" wailed Henry.

Then **Horrid Henry** saw a **HORRIBLE** sight. Behind Aunt Ruby's back, Steve and Bill were

covering their mouths and laughing.
Henry realised the **TERRIBLE**
truth. Bill and Steve had tricked him.
They'd broken the bed. And now he'd
got the blame.

"BUT I DIDN'T BREAK IT!"
screamed Henry.

"Yes you did, Henry," said Peter.
"I saw you."

AAAARRRRGGGGHHHH!

Horrid Henry leapt at Peter. He was
a *storm god* hurling thunderbolts at a
foolish mortal.

"AAAIIIEEEEEE!" squealed

Perfect Peter.

"Henry! Stop it!" shrieked Mum. "Leave your brother alone."

NAH NAH NE NAH NAH, mouthed Steve behind Aunt Ruby's back.

"Isn't it *lovely* how nicely the boys are playing together?" said Aunt Ruby.

"Yes, isn't it?" said Mum.

"Not surprising," said Aunt Ruby, beaming. "After all, Steve is such a polite, friendly boy, I've never met anyone who didn't love him."

Snore! Snore! Snore!

Horrid Henry lay on a mattress listening to hideous snoring sounds. He'd stayed awake for hours, just in case they tried anything **HORRIBLE**, like pouring water on his head, or stuffing frogs in his bed. Which was what he was going to do to Peter, the moment he got home.

Henry had just spent the most horrible Saturday of his life. He'd *begged* to go to the **PAINTBALLING** party. He'd *pleaded* to go to the paintballing

party. He'd **SCREAMED** about going
to the paintballing party. But no. His
MEAN, HORRIBLE parents wouldn't
budge. And it was all Steve and Bill's
fault.

They'd tripped him going down the stairs.
They'd kicked him under the table
at dinner (and then complained that
he was kicking them). And every time
Aunt Ruby's back was turned they
stuck out their tongues and jeered:

"We're going PAINTBALLING, and you're not."

He had to get to that party. And he had to be revenged. But how? How? His two arch-enemies had banded together and struck the first blow.

Could he **booby-trap** their beds and remove a few slats? Unfortunately, everyone would know he'd done it and he'd be in even more trouble than he was now.

Scare them? Tell them there was a **MONSTER** under the bed? Hmmm. He knew Steve was as big a scaredy cat as Peter. But he'd already done that once. He didn't think Steve would fall for it again.

Get them into trouble? Turn them against each other? Steal their best toys and hide them? Hmmm. Hmmm. **Horrid Henry** thought and thought.

He had to be revenged. He had to.

TWEET TWEET. It was Sunday morning. The birds were singing. The sun was shining. The—

Yank!

Bossy Bill and STUCK-UP STEVE pulled off his duvet.

"Nah na ne nah nah, we-ee beat you," crowed Bill.

"Nah na ne nah nah, we got you into trouble," crowed Steve.

Horrid Henry scowled. Time to put **Operation Revenge** into action.

"Bill thinks you're bossy, Steve," said Henry. "He told me."

"Didn't," said Bossy Bill.

"And Steve thinks you're stuck-up, Bill," added Henry sweetly.

"No I don't," said Steve.

"Then why'd you tell me that?" said Horrid Henry.

Steve stuck his nose in the air.

"Nice try, Henry, you big loser," said STUCK-UP STEVE. "Just ignore him, Bill."

"Henry, it's not nice to tell lies," said Perfect Peter.

"Shut up, WORM," snarled Horrid Henry.

RATS.

Time for plan B.

Except he didn't have a plan B.

"I can't wait for Tim's party," said

Bossy Bill. "You never know what's going to happen."

"Yeah, remember when he told us he was having a *pirate party* and instead we went to the *Wild West Theme Park!*" said Steve.

"Or when he said we were having a sleepover, and instead we all went to a **MANIC BUZZARDS** concert."

"And Tim gives the best party bags. Last year everyone got a *Deluxe Demon Dagger Sabre*," said Steve. "Wonder what he'll give this year? Oh, I forgot, Henry won't be coming to the party."

"Too bad you can't come, Henry," sneered Bossy Bill.

"Yeah, too bad," sneered Stuck-Up Steve. "Not."

ARRRRGGGHH. Horrid Henry's blood boiled. He couldn't decide what was worse, listening to them **CROW** about having got him into so much trouble, or brag about the great **PARTY** they were going to and he wasn't.

"I can't wait to find out what surprises he'll have in store this year," said Bill.

"Yeah," said Steve.

Who cares? thought **Horrid Henry**. Unless Tim was planning to throw Bill and Steve into a **shark tank**. That would be a nice surprise. Unless of course . . . And then suddenly Horrid Henry had a *brilliant*, **SPECTACULAR** idea. It was so *brilliant*, and so **SPECTACULAR**, that for a moment he wondered whether

he could stop himself from *flinging* open the window and shouting his plan out loud. Oh wow. Oh wow. It was risky.

It was dangerous. But if it worked, he would have the best revenge ever in the history of the **WORLD**. No, the history of the **SOLAR SYSTEM**. No, the history of the **UNIVERSE!**

It was an hour before the party. **Horrid Henry** was counting the seconds until he could escape.

Aunt Ruby popped her head round the door *waving* an envelope.

"Letter for you boys," she said.

Steve **SNATCHED** it and tore it open.

Dear Steve and Bill

Party of the year update.
Everyone must come to my house
wearing pyjamas (you'll find
out why later, but don't be
surprised if we all end up in
a film — shhhh). It'll be a real
laugh. Make sure to bring
your favourite soft toys, too,
and wear your fluffiest
slippers. Hollywood, here
we come!

Tim

"He must be planning something amazing," said Bill.

"I bet we're all going to be acting in a film!" said Steve.

"Yeah!" said Bill.

"Too bad you won't, Henry," said STUCK-UP STEVE.

"You're so LUCKY," said Henry. "I wish I were going."

Mum looked at Dad.

Dad looked at Mum.

Henry held his breath.

"Well, you can't, Henry, and that's final," said Mum.

"IT'S SO UNFAIR!" shrieked Henry.

Henry's parents dropped Steve and Bill off at Tim's party on their way home. Steve was in his blue bunny pyjamas and blue bunny fluffy slippers, and clutching a panda.

Bill was in his yellow duckling pyjamas and yellow duckling fluffy slippers, and clutching his monkey.

"Shame you can't come, Henry," said Steve, smirking. "But we'll be sure to tell you all about it."

"Do," said Henry, as Mum drove off.

Horrid Henry heard squeals of laughter at Hoity-Toity Tim's front door. Bill and Steve stood frozen. Then they started to wave frantically at the car.

"Are they saying something?" said Mum, glancing in the rear-view mirror.

"Nah, just waving goodbye," said Horrid Henry. He rolled down his window.

"Have fun, guys!"

HORRID HENRY'S

BAD BOOK

"Henry. Get down here."

"Henry. We're waiting for you."

"I'm READING!" bellowed Horrid Henry.

How could he go out with his mean, HORRIBLE parents before he found out what Evil Evie would do next?

Evil Evie came up with the best tricks. The time she pretended to be allergic to vegetables! Or put slugs in her sister's slippers for April Fool's Day! Or swapped her parents. Or

saved the planet by
refusing to take baths.

Or won the **LOTTERY**
and spent every penny
on toys and chocolate. Or rode in the
car with a pot of lasagne on her lap
and accidentally took the lid off . . .
WOW.

Why couldn't he have a *brilliant*
sister like **Evie** instead of a waste of
space **WOFMY** T̄oAD brother like Peter?

"Not those awful books again," said Dad.

"Can't you find anything better to
read?" said Mum.

"These are the *best books ever*," said Horrid Henry.

"Too mean," said Mum.

"Too aggressive," said Dad.

Horrid Henry sighed.

First, his parents complained that he only read comics. Then, after he'd discovered the *best books ever* in the history of the universe and couldn't stop reading them over and over and over again, and even bought them with his own **PRECIOUS** pocket money, his parents complained that they hated the Evil Evie series.

"Such a bad example," said Mum.

"They put ideas into his head," said Dad.

"Why can't you read books about good children who always obey their parents?" they moaned.

Horrid Henry rolled his eyes. Wasn't reading meant to be about **FUN** and **adventure** and *escape?* He got enough real life in real life.

Horrid Henry loved **Evil Evie**.

Rude Ralph loved **Evil Evie**.

MOODY MARGARET loved Evil Evie.

In fact, **EVERYONE** at school loved Evil Evie.

Even **MISS BATTLE-AXE** loved the Evil Evie books and read her adventures out loud every day during story-time. Evil Evie and the Roaring Rogues. Evil Evie and the Tyrant Teacher.

Evil Evie and the Mad Scientist. Evil Evie, Pirate Queen.

They were definitely the funniest books ever.

Horrid Henry could win any Evil Evie competition. He knew everything about her.

Her favourite vegetable: **ketchup**.

Her catch-phrase: **BUZZ OFF, ~~BANANA-HEAD~~**.

Her favourite word: *swashbuckling*.

Her favourite colour: purple (just like his).

Her favourite TV

programme: Robot Riot.

Her *evilest* enemies: Rotten Robert, the **MONSTER** next door, and Snobby Bobby, her stuck-up cousin.

Her secret job: Spy Assassin.

Her **FOUL** sister: Wilting Willa, an infant fiend in training.

Her pet rat: Doris.

Her hometown: Rudeville.

Her **MEAN, HORRIBLE** parents. Hmmm, they didn't appear to have names. Probably because they were so old they'd forgotten them, thought Horrid Henry.

Evil Evie was **Horrid Henry's** Mastermind subject.

Best of all, every time Henry got into trouble, he blamed Evil Evie.

"Evie did that," he squealed when Mum told him off for poking Peter.

"Evie did that," he shrieked when Dad told him off for calling Peter names.

"Evie did that," lied Henry, when Mum and Dad told him off for calling the police when **MISS BATTLE-AXE** refused to give him sweets.

After all, his parents hadn't read

the Evil Evie
books, had
they? How
would they
know?

Tee hee.

"Mum!"

squealed Peter. "Henry called me
wimpadoodle and **wibble wobble
pants**."

"Stop being **HORRID**, Henry,"
said Mum.

"Henry was never **HORRID**
until he started reading those

horrible
books,"
said
Dad.

"Those books are a bad influence," said Mum. "He always played *nicely* with Peter before."

"Really?" said Grandma. "I don't remember that."

From next door came the sound of slapping.

"**I HATE YOU**, Susan," screamed Margaret.

"**I hate you more**," screamed Susan.

Moody Margaret's mum leaned over the garden wall.

"You know how my little Maggie Moo Moo has always been the sweetest, kindest, QUIETEST child ever," said her mother. "A jewel. Perfect in every way. Well, ever since she discovered Evil Evie she's become . . . a total **TERROR**."

"Henry too," said Mum. "I'm sure he'd play beautifully with his brother if those books hadn't put ideas into his head."

"I'm sick and tired of these

TERRIBLE books," said Margaret's mother. "Margaret's become so MOODY since she started reading them."

Horrid Henry looked up from his book, Evil Evie Stings the Scorpion.

"Margaret's been a moody old grouch since she was a tadpole," said Henry.

"Don't be HORRID, Henry," said Mum.

"I never read Evil Evie," said Peter. "I'd much rather read about good children."

"Quite right, Peter," said Mum.

Horrid Henry pounced.

He was a giant mosquito *dive-bombing* for his supper.

"Aiieeeeee!" squealed Peter. "Henry pinched me."

"**Evil Evie** did that to her sister," said Horrid Henry. "I was just copying her."

Tee hee. **Evil Evie** was the best get-out-of-jail-free card ever.

Horrid Henry walked into his bedroom after a long day at school.

Phew.

Finally, a chance to relax on his bed with a favourite **Evil Evie**, maybe **Evil Evie** and the Dastardly Demon—

Huh?

His special Evil Evie bookcase was empty.

"Where are my **Evil Evie** books?" shrieked Henry. "Someone's stolen them."

"Banned," said Mum, coming into the room.

"Banned," said Dad. "We're sick and tired of your **HORRID** copy-cat behaviour."

Oops.

Horrid Henry hadn't thought of that. He thought he'd been brilliant blaming everything on Evie. And now his brilliance had backfired.

"But I want to read," wailed Horrid Henry.

"And that's why we've got a present for you, Henry," said Mum. "The fabulous *Gallant Gary* series. Much better than Evil Evie. Margaret's mum recommended them."

She handed Henry a book with a sparkling silver cover. There was a picture of a boy holding a tea towel, with a halo framing his brown curls.

"Gallant . . . Gary?" said Horrid Henry. He read the story titles.

BLECCCCCHHH.

Horrid Henry opened the book as if
it were **radioactive** and flicked through
the *grisly* pages.

There was *Gallant Gary* helping an old lady across the street.

There was *Gallant Gary* telling his mum to rest her feet while he cleared the table and did loads of chores.

There was *Gallant Gary* playing catch with his adorable younger brother Little Larry.

BLECCCCCHHH.

Horrid Henry slammed the book shut.

UGGGH.

Didn't he have enough goody goodies in his life with Peter?

"These stories are **BORING**," said Henry. "I want my Evil Evie books back."

"Maybe you'll learn something," said Mum.

"Maybe you'll stop being so **HORRID**," said Dad.

"Why don't you copy *Gary?*" said Mum. "That would be wonderful."

"**NO!**" screamed Henry.

At lunchtime **Horrid Henry** went
to his school library. Why hadn't he
thought of this before? TRALALA, he'd
check out some **Evil Evie** books and
cover them with *Gallant Gary* covers.
TRALALA, a trick worthy of Evie herself . . .

What?

The **Evil Evie** shelf was empty.

"All the **Evil Evie** books are checked
out, I'm afraid," said the librarian,
Beaming Bea. "I have lots of *Gallant
Gary* if you want to try something new."

"**NOOOOOOO**," said Horrid Henry. "I
want to read **Evil Evie!!**"

"You and everyone else," said the librarian.

He had to get his books back. He had to. He couldn't get to sleep without an **Evil Evie** book. He couldn't relax after school without an **Evil Evie** book.

Why had he ever blamed **Evie** for being **HORRID?** What would **Evie** do in this dreadful situation?

And then suddenly **Horrid Henry** had a *brilliant*, **SPECTACULAR**

idea. It was
so *brilliant*, and so
SPECTACULAR,
that Henry started
dancing around the
library, whooping and
cheering.

"Shhh," said Beaming Bea, frowning.

What was it Mum had said? Why
didn't he copy Gary?

Copy *Gallant Gary*, thought Henry.
Copy *Gallant Gary*. **BOY** could he copy
Gallant Gary.

On their way to the park **Horrid Henry** grabbed Grandma and tugged on her arm.

"I'm helping you cross the road," he shouted.

"But I don't want to cross the road," said Grandma.

"Too bad," said Henry, *yanking* her. "You're

an old lady and you're crossing."

"HELP!" squealed Grandma.

"Henry, stop that at once," shouted Mum.

Henry stopped. "But I'm only copying *Gary*, like you said. He's always helping old ladies cross the road."

Mum opened her mouth and then closed it.

SQUELCH

SQUERCH.

"Mum!" squealed Peter.

Mum ran into the sitting room. Great globs of **SOAPY SUDS** bubbled from the carpet up to Peter's knees.

"What's going on?" said Mum. "Henry! What have you done?" she said, looking at the **bubbling** carpet.

"I was just copying *Gary*," said Henry, squirting more shampoo. "I know you wanted to shampoo the carpet and I was trying to help you with your chores, just like *Gary*."

"Stop," said Mum, as her feet sank in the suds. "Uhhm, thank you Henry, that's enough."

That night, after supper, Horrid Henry leapt to his feet.

"I'll clear," said Horrid Henry, gathering all the dirty plates and heading towards the kitchen.

CRASH SMASH

Broken plates cascaded round the floor.

"Henry!" shouted Dad.

"I'm copying *Gary*, just like you said," said Henry. "He always clears the table."

"Oh," said Mum.

"Oh," said Dad.

"C'mon, Peter, let's play catch in the garden," said Horrid Henry.

Perfect Peter stared. Henry never offered to play with him.

Mum smiled. "Yes, go on, Peter," she said.

"Just like *Gallant Gary*, and Little Larry," said Henry, hurling the ball.

The ball torpedoed through the kitchen window.

CRASH.

Glass splinters flew everywhere as the window shattered.

"HENRY!" screamed Mum and Dad.

"I'm so sorry," said Horrid Henry. "I was just copying *Gary*. He and Little Larry are always playing catch."

Mum looked at Dad.

Dad looked at Mum.

They stared at the **~~BROKEN~~** window, the **soapy** carpet and the

smashed dishes.

"Don't worry," said Horrid Henry. "I'll keep copying *Gary*, just like you said."

"Oh," said Mum.

"Oh," said Dad.

Horrid Henry came home from school the next day and walked slowly up to his bedroom. No . No chance to relax with an **Evil Evie** book—

Henry stared. His special bookshelf was full. Packed to the brim with **Evil**

Evie books.

Evil Evie was back. *Gary* was gone.

YIPPEE!!!!!!

Horrid Henry picked up his favourite book and lay back on his bed.

He turned to the first page and began to read.

Evie was evil.

Everyone said so, even her mother.

HORRID HENRY

FRIGHT NIGHT

Turn the page for
lots of fun games
and activities!

Morse Code

HENRY LOVES TRICK OR TREATING — ESPECIALLY THE
TRICKS! LAST YEAR, MUM FOUND HIS LIST OF TRICKS
AND HE GOT IN SO MUCH TROUBLE. HE'S NOT LETTING
THAT HAPPEN AGAIN! THAT'S WHY HE'S WRITTEN
THEM ALL IN CODE — MORSE CODE TO BE EXACT!

A = ·−   J = ·−−−   S = ···
B = −···   K = −·−   T = −
C = −·−·   L = ·−··   U = ··−
D = −··   M = −−   V = ···−
E = ·   N = −·   W = ·−−
F = ··−·   O = −−−   X = −··−
G = −−·   P = ·−−·   Y = −·−−
H = ····   Q = −−·−   Z = −−··
I = ··   R = ·−·

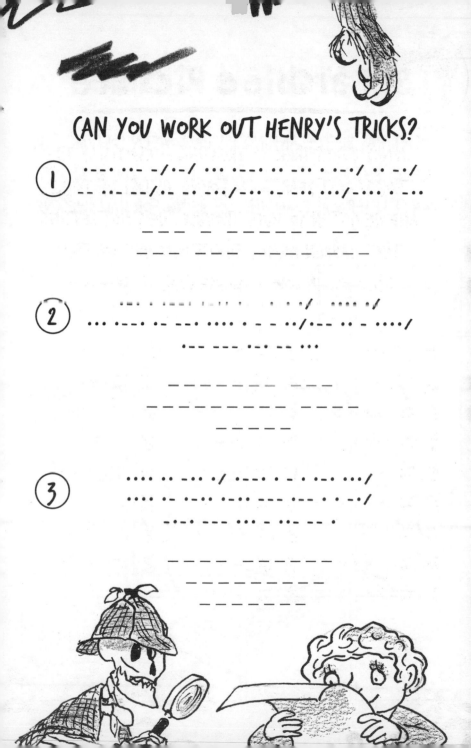

CAN YOU WORK OUT HENRY'S TRICKS?

1 ·--· ··· -/·-/ ··· ·--- ·· ··· · ·--/ ·· --·/
-- ··· --/·· -· ··/-·· ·· -- ··· ···/-··· · ·--

--- - ------ --
--- --- ---- ---

2 ··-· · ·--· ···· · · · ·/ ···· ·/
··· ·--· ·· ·· --- ···· · - -- ··/·-- ·· - ···/
·-- --- ·-- -- ···

------- ---
--------- ----
-----

3 ···· ·· -·· ·/ ·--· · ·· ·-- ···/
···· ·· ·-·· ·-·· --- ·-- ·· ·--/
·-·· --- ·· - ·· -- ·

---- ------

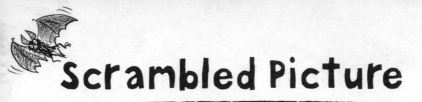

Scrambled Picture

PETER HAS BEEN PLANNING HIS HALLOWEEN COSTUME FOR
WEEKS BUT NOW IT'S ALL SCRAMBLED. CAN YOU WORK OUT
WHAT PETER WAS PLANNING ON BEING FOR HALLOWE'EN?

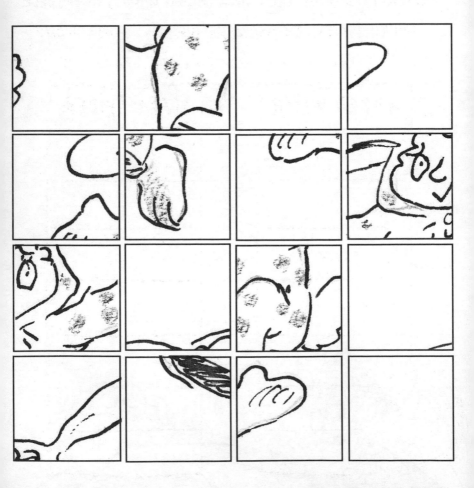

Brain Teasers

HENRY AND MARGARET ARE COMPETING TO SEE WHO IS SMARTEST BY COMPLETING THE BRAINTEASERS BELOW. ALL THEY HAVE TO DO IS MAKE AS MANY WORDS FROM THE LETTERS IN EACH OF THESE HALLOWE'EN GHOULS AS POSSIBLE – WHICH TEASER CAN YOU MAKE THE MOST WORDS FROM?

WICKED WITCH

SCARY SPIDER

Crossword!

HENRY LOVES HALLOWE'EN – IT'S THE BEST TIME OF THE YEAR! CAN YOU SOLVE THIS CROSSWORD ALL ABOUT HENRY'S FAVOURITE DAY?

ACROSS

1. SOMETHING THAT SAYS 'BOO'
5. WEAR THIS TO SCARE PEOPLE
7. WHAT A WITCH USES TO MAKE POTIONS
8. A COSTUME THAT'S BLACK AND WHITE
9. WHAT ZOMBIES EAT

DOWN

2. NOT A TRICK BUT A...
3. EAT A LOT OF THIS SWEET TREAT
4. AN EASY COSTUME – ALL YOU NEED IS TOILET PAPER!
6. A JACK-O-LANTERN
9. WHAT A VAMPIRE TURNS INTO

Devil's in the Detail

HENRY LOVED HIS DEVIL COSTUME BUT THE ONLY
PHOTO HE HAS WAS RIPPED IN HALF.
FILL IN THE REST OF THE PICTURE.

Sudoku

PETER HAS DECIDED TO MAKE ONE OF HIS FAVOURITE GAMES HALLOWE'EN THEMED! CAN YOU SOLVE THESE SPOOKY SUDOKUS? YOU CAN'T HAVE THE SAME NUMBER IN A ROW, COLUMN OR BOX MORE THAN ONCE!

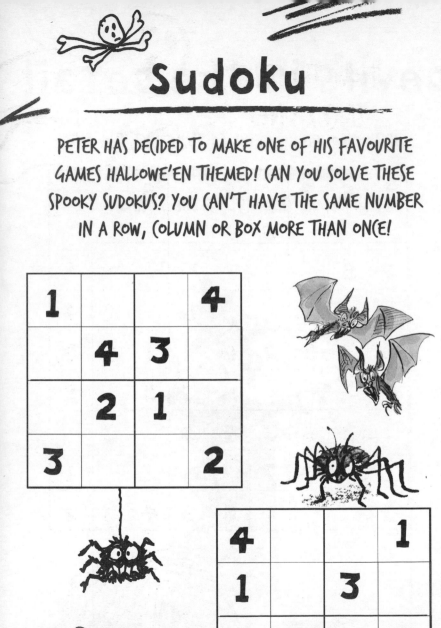

Puzzle 1:

1			4
	4	3	
	2	1	
3			2

Puzzle 2:

4			1
1		3	
	4		3
3			2

1	6	7		2		8		
			6	1				
2	8							
					5		2	4
8	3	5	2	6	4	1	9	7
4					3	5		8
	2	8	3	4	1		5	
		3	7					1
5				8	6	4	3	2

Hallowe'en Costume

HENRY HAS TO FIND OUT WHAT MARGARET IS DRESSING UP AS FOR HALLOWE'EN – ONCE THEY BOTH WENT AS ZOMBIES AND HE CAN'T RISK THAT AGAIN! CAN YOU JOIN THE DOTS TO FIND OUT WHAT HER COSTUME WILL BE?

Who Am I?

PETER SAYS HE CAN BEAT HENRY AT ANY QUIZ –
HA! NO ONE KNOWS HALLOWE'EN LIKE HENRY DOES.
IT'S ONLY THE BEST TIME OF THE YEAR! THERE'S
NO WAY PETER IS BEATING HIM AT THIS ONE . . .

CAN YOU WORK OUT WHO EVERYONE IS ?

I'm magic but I don't have a broom. The most famous of us is probably Merlin...he gets all the attention!

(_ _ _ _ _ _)

I'm...pretty...slow...*but...I...will...get...to...the...brains...one...day...*

(_ _ _ _ _ _)

Leave me alone! Open my sarcophagus and you're definitely getting cursed!

(_ _ _ _ _)

Is that...is that a full moon? *NOOOOOO! GRRRAAAAAHHHHH!*

(_ _ _ _ _ _ _ _)

I'm quite sleepy actually, would you mind closing the coffin door on your way out?

(_ _ _ _ _ _ _)

The ULTIMATE Horrid Henry Quiz

DO YOU THINK YOU KNOW ALL THERE IS TO KNOW ABOUT HORRID HENRY? TIME TO FIND OUT IF YOU'RE A CLEVER CLARE OR A BEEFY BERT!

1. What is Horrid Henry's brother called?
   a) Perfect Peter   ○
   b) Funny Fred   ○
   c) Cheeky Charlie   ○

2. Who is Miss Lovely?
   a) The babysitter   ○
   b) The nurse   ○
   c) A teacher   ○

3. Who is Margaret's best friend?
   a) Aerobic Al   ○
   b) Gorgeous Gurinder   ○
   c) Sour Susan   ○

4. What is Peter's favourite food?
   a) Ice cream   ○
   b) Biscuits   ○
   c) Vegetables   ○

5. Who is the greatest enemy of The Secret Club?
a) The Sasquatch Squad ◯
b) The Purple Hand Gang ◯
c) The Sneaky Sneak Team ◯

6. What is Peter's cat called?
a) Scruffy ◯
b) Cuddly ◯
c) Fluffy ◯

7. What's Miss Battle-Axe's least favourite thing?
a) Chocolate ◯
b) Children ◯
c) Quiet ◯

8. Which team is Moody Margaret captain of?
a) Hockey ◯
b) Netball ◯
c) Football ◯

9. What's the name of Peter's club?
a) The Best Boy's Club ◯
b) The Good Boy Collective ◯
c) The Smart Boy Group ◯

10. Who are Henry's favourite band?
a) The Angry Pigeon Men ◯
b) The Killer Boys Rats ◯
c) The Furious Spider People ◯

Fact File

HENRY HAD TO FILL IN A FACT SHEET FOR SCHOOL. TAKE A LOOK!

BEST FRIEND:	RUDE RALPH
FAVOURITE FOOD:	CHOCOLATE
WORST FOOD:	LUMPY SURPRISE WITH LUMPS
	FROM THE DEMON DINNER LADY
BEST SUBJECT:	LUNCH
WORST SUBJECT:	ALL THE OTHERS

CAN YOU FILL IN YOUR OWN?

BEST FRIEND:	
FAVOURITE FOOD:	
WORST FOOD:	
BEST SUBJECT:	
WORST SUBJECT:	

Answers

Morse Code

1. PUT A SPIDER IN MUM AND DAD'S BED
2. REPLACE THE SPAGHETTI WITH WORMS
3. HIDE PETER'S HALLOWEEN COSTUME

Scrambled Picture

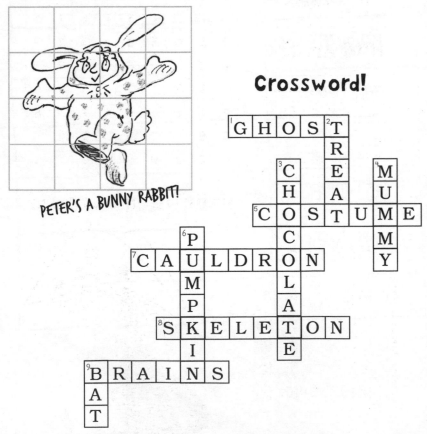

PETER'S A BUNNY RABBIT!

Crossword!

Devil's in the Detail

Sudoku

1	3	2	4
2	4	3	1
4	2	1	3
3	1	4	2

4	3	2	1
1	2	3	4
2	4	1	3
3	1	4	2

1	6	7	5	2	9	8	4	3
3	5	4	6	1	8	2	7	9
2	8	9	4	3	7	6	1	5
7	1	6	8	9	5	3	2	4
8	3	5	2	6	4	1	9	7
4	9	2	1	7	3	5	6	8
9	2	8	3	4	1	7	5	6
6	4	3	7	5	2	9	8	1
5	7	1	9	8	6	4	3	2

Who Am I?

- WIZARD
- ZOMBIE
- MUMMY
- WEREWOLF
- VAMPIRE

Hallowe'en Costume

Ultimate Quiz

1.	(a)	6.	(c)
2.	(c)	7.	(b)
3.	(c)	8.	(c)
4.	(c)	9.	(a)
5.	(b)	10.	(b)

COLLECT ALL THE HORRID HENRY STORYBOOKS!

Horrid Henry
Horrid Henry: Secret Club
Horrid Henry: Tricking the Tooth Fairy
Horrid Henry: Nits Nits Nits!
Horrid Henry: Get Rich Quick
Horrid Henry: The Haunted House
Horrid Henry: The Mummy's Curse
Horrid Henry: Perfect Revenge
Horrid Henry: Bogey Babysitter
Horrid Henry: Stinkbombs!
Horrid Henry: Underpants Panic
Horrid Henry: The Queen's Visit
Horrid Henry: Mega-Mean Time Machine
Horrid Henry: Football Fiend
Horrid Henry: Christmas Cracker
Horrid Henry: Abominable Snowman
Horrid Henry: Bank Robber
Horrid Henry: Waking the Dead
Horrid Henry: Rock Star
Horrid Henry: Zombie Vampire
Horrid Henry: Monster Movie
Horrid Henry: Nightmare!
Horrid Henry: Krazy Ketchup
Horrid Henry: Cannibal Curse
Horrid Henry: Up, Up and Away